LEGENDS OF FERNANDO OF NORONHA AND OTHER STORIES

Legends of Fernando of Noronha and other stories

ALDIVAN TORRES

Canary Of Joy

Contents

1 Legends of Fernando of Noronha and Other Stories   1

1

Legends of Fernando of Noronha and Other Stories

Legends of Fernando of Noronha and other stories
Aldivan Torres

Author: Aldivan Torres
©2020- Aldivan Torres
All rights reserved.
Series: Fables   of   the   Universe

This book, including all parts of it, is copyrighted and may not be reproduced without permission of the author, resold or transferred.

Aldivan Torres, a natural from Brazil, is a consolidated writer in various genres. So far, it has titles published in dozens of languages. Since early, he's always been a lover of the art of writing, consolidated a professional career from the second semester of 2013. You wait with your writings to contribute to Brazilian culture, awakening the pleasure of reading in those who are not yet in habit. Your mission is to conquer the heart of each of your readers. In addition to literature, its main tastes are music, travel, friends, family and the very pleasure of living. For literature, equality, fraternity, justice, dignity, and honor of human being always" is his motto.

Legends of Fernando of Noronha and Other Stories
Dedication and thanks
The legend of Alamoa
The gypsy
Roof man
Federal prison
The Giants of Fernando of Noronha
The Golden Pot Woman
Midnight giant
The lost treasure
The crippled, teeth-free boy
The Sea Monster
The Heavy Woman
forest
The haunted house
The monster of the forest
The Pearl Island in Polynesia
A paradise in the middle of the sea
On the island of Ascension
The arrival to the island

Dedication and thanks

I dedicate this job to God, my family, my journey companions and my readers. I wouldn't be anything without you. Each line written has a little of this incentive and the Brazilian claw. We are a battling, full of dreams that still have to make this country the best in the world.

I appreciate my gift, the good times I lived, the bad times that have made me grow, the books read, the good comments, the critics pointing flaws, at last, I thank every person who is part of my life. I'm a meeting of thoughts and un-

certainty being led to destiny. This destiny is the house of each of my followers. How nice to be a part of your life.

All stories deserve to be told, whether they're important or not. These are the memories that remain forever and eternize man. So don't search for material goods. Search the kingdom of God first, and all the other things will be given to you by earnings.

The legend of Alamoa

A group of pirates sails several days across the ocean carrying the fruits of their last works. It's a pretty tight, fun, decisive group. They've been together for years on many adventures that they could stand out their union and mutual cooperation. They were real pirates in their intrinsic essence.

When he approaches the archipelago of Fernando of Noronha, they start talking to each other.

"The night is coming and the body won't relax. What should we do now, dear sailors? He questioned the captain, a tall, bearded, wrinkled with wrinkles due to age.

"I think we can dock right now. That way, we can spend the quietest night, suggested Pietro, a strong, delegate brown, one of the sailors.

"Good idea. But at what point? Anybody thinks of anything? Has been wrapped up the captain.

"The island of Fernando of Noronha is near here. It's the only place we can dock. But it's also a very dangerous place, full of supernatural creatures. What do you think? He suggested Herbert, a blonde with a ponytail, one of the most experienced crewmen.

"I think that's a big nonsense. Are we pirates or not? That doesn't scare me, affirming one of the women.

"These women make me proud. I wanted to be like them. I'm afraid of these legends speak the group cook.

"This is expected. What you lack in courage, leaves in skill in the kitchen. That's why your part of our team, you've affirmed the captain.

"Thank you for your compliments, Captain. I promise to improve more and more and more and more the cook has returned.

~" We're going to Fernando of Noronha to make history. I'm sure it'll be all right decided the captain.

"So be it, they wished the other members.

The ship has been directed to the island. In each of them, there was a feeling of adventure, fear and expectation. What would happen? Were such stories true? The only certainty they had was that they would face every obstacle in the way. They were proud of themselves for being so brave. So, they were doing the fame of the most feared pirates in the ocean.

"I can see the island. We're coming, gentlemen! Announced one of them.

There's a fuss on the ship and everyone cooperates for a better arrival. In a few minutes, they dock the ship by the sea and everyone comes down. The island was quiet and cold as usual. A beauty show for everyone who was there. The captain resumes the dialogue:

"Now we're on dry land. Men, head for the woods. Go get some food and wood to build a fire. We need to build a cabin too. She'll be shelter for all of us because there are a lot of fierce animals around here. Women, clear the ground around while we wait for the arrival of our dear sailors.

"Okay. We're going to fulfill the order, sir.

What a dedicated team! It's at times when I feel a great pride.

The groups have separated aiming to follow the boss's orders. The island of Fernando of Noronha breathed air of tranquility, sea and mystery. Ali, anything could happen. A while later, the groups return with the tasks accomplished.

"Finally, the fire and tents are ready. Now, we need to prepare the food suggested the captain.

"I'll do it immediately, promised the cook.

"That's how it was done. The cook started cooking delicious food. The rest of us were resting on the floor of exhausting trip.

"What a lovely smell! These fish look very tasty.

"Thank you, boss! I'm trying to provide you with a good meal, you've claimed the cook.

"I know. In addition to the supernatural creatures the island harbors, they say she is thirsty for incalculable treasures informed Herbert.

"This is very good. Are you willing to help me get this treasure, sailor? He asked the captain.

"What am I not doing for my dear boss? Yes, I am able to risk my own life.

"I'm glad you decided. You just have to fulfill the pirate's oath; the action of a pirate protects others. (Captain)

"I promise my work will be done that way. (Herbert)

"The food is ready! Come and eat, you bunch! (cook)

Everyone gathered around the fire. In the distance, you could hear terrifying wolves' howls. The night was moving forward.

"As always, the food is delicious. Where do you get your talent, dear servant? (Captain)

"I believe I learned from my mother. May she rest in peace in good place. Since childhood, she taught me a lot of recipes. With this, I like the cooking.

"Bless your mother. You've left us a wonderful, competent, delicate person. (Rainy, one of the women)

"Thank you, mate. I'll try to serve them as best I can. I'm glad to be pleasant.

"All you need is to have a little more courage. (Bella, another woman)

"You're right. But is there someone perfect in this world? (cook)

"Nobody. I was just kidding. You don't have to try to change. You're useful enough for us. (Bella)

"Thank you! (cook)

The conversation continued on several matters and with that time was passing. Then the captain announced:

"It's time for bed. Can you take care of us, Pietro?

"Yes. Absolutely. You can go to sleep peacefully. Nothing will harm them.

The entire crew went to sleep while the guard took care of everyone. Meanwhile, the night was moving further. Near midnight, a strange figure approached him.

"Good night, good gentleman. Can you help me?

"What do you want, dear lady? What are you doing alone on this cold night?

"I'm an island resident and I've heard your conversation. You seek the treasure?

"Yes. How can you help me?

"I know exactly where the money is. I just can't get it because I'm scared.

"Interesting. What's your proposal?

'Let's get the treasure together. As soon as we get it, we'll split the prize.

"This sounds like a good idea. But how am I supposed to leave my team without a guard?

"Nothing's going to happen to them. This is a very quiet area. Fire will scare the dangerous animals. Besides, your captain's greatest wish is the treasure. Have you thought about his joy when he finds out you've got it? You're definitely getting promoted.

"It's going to be a big surprise. What are we waiting for? Take us to the treasure site.

"All right! We're going right now!

The dynamic duo started walking and crossed the island. They make a strategic stop at Alamoa peak.

"They say Alamoa's peak is too dangerous. Should we continue? (Pietro)

"Do you still believe in these beliefs? Forget superstition and we'll keep walking. The treasure awaits us. (Lady)

"Have you lived here long?

"I'm a natural here. This place is blessed by God. It's a shame that many people kick out tourists with false rumors.

'What's the meaning of this?

'Axe Competition. This is paradise. People are selfish and centralized.

"And you, aren't you?

"We're talking business. You want the treasure?

"Of course, I do.

~" All right.

The walk goes on for a while. Coming to the top, the strange figure has become a mixture of demon and blonde woman.

"We're here! Where's the treasure? (Pietro)

"In your silly mind.

'Who are you?

"I am Alamoa, the goddess of the island. You invaded my space. Now, you will pay with your own life for the peace of your colleagues.

The devil attacked the man and devoured him. Another victim of this legendary figure. The saying goes, "In the world, there is everything and we must not doubt it."

The gypsy

A group of gypsies landed on Fernando's Island of Noronha after they were kicked off the mainland.

"We're here. This is now our land. We were kicked off the mainland for racial cleaning. However, we are much more than the white man thinks. We are messengers of Bel, the Almighty God.

"That's right, sister. We don't need the white man. We have the strength of the spirit that leads our dreams. Furthermore, we're no better or worse than anyone. We consider this exile as a learning. Let's forget the sorrows, the pain, and the disfavors passed.

"We'll consider this exile as a learning. Let's forget the sorrows, pain and "disgust of the past.

"We need to, for, to evolve in our quest for God. Let him help us.

"Let it be done.

Talking on the island beach at sundown.

"What a wonderful island. Having been kicked off the mainland doesn't seem to have been a bad idea. I feel my strength pulsing and rejuvenating. I feel, therefore, complete.

"Me too, sister. We need to be prepared to receive visitors at night.

"Is there anyone else here on this lost island?

'Yes, a Dutch pirate and a priest.

"No women? Am I safe here?

'Yes, you are. What's wrong with that? I know you can defend yourself.

"It's true. I'm a master of seduction and spiritual control. There is no man who does not succumb to my charms. I'm ready for whatever comes and goes!

"This is the way to talk, sister. I'll be back in a little while. I need to get us some wood and food.

"Okay. Meanwhile, I'm going to meditate a little.

The gypsy goes into a state of meditation. A mild calm fills the whole environment in the thunder and lightning.

"My mighty gods, entities that blow from there to here, I ask you for inspiration and protection in the days. Be friends with my friends and enemy of my enemies. Anyway, fate prevails in my life.

The gypsy's brother came and built the cabin.

"The cabin is ready!

"Great! Good job, brother.

Then a priest and a pirate came to keep you company and talk a little.

"We've come to greet our new neighbors. May the peace of Christ be with you! (Father)

'Appreciated, Father. I wish you the same. (Gypsy)

"May the good spirits protect you.

'Thank you, buddy. This is Captain Willy, a pirate friend who's been keeping me company for many years.

"Welcome, Willy! (Gypsy)

"Be my guest, buddy! (Brother)

"I appreciate your hospitality. I love this place, but I feel extremely alone. (Willy)

"But don't you have the priest? (Brother)

"Not to want to disregard my colleague, it's not the same. Being around a woman seems to change me completely. (Willy)

"I see. But let's keep our distance. Respect is first. (Gypsy)

"Of course, Miss. At no time, I disrespected you, even though you have so many attributes. (Willy)

'Thank goodness.

"Besides, I'm here to defend you. (Brother)

"Thanks for the support, brother. (Gypsy)

"Be calm. We came for peace. (Father)

"Shall we eat then? They must be hungry.

"You nailed it, dear. (Willy)

The quartet entered the cabin. Dinner was served and then resumed the conversation.

"How long have you been on the island? (Brother)

"Three years ago. We are the guardians of this place for the government. You know, we don't compact with our superiors' decision. For us, gypsies are very kind and intelligent beings. We're brothers in Christ.

"Your kind, Father. To others, we're scum. We're a rotten thing that can be thrown away. It's painful that exclusion because it hurts the soul. We're also children of the same God.

"What they want is for us to die here. You may even get that, but those responsible won't get away with it. (Brother)

"Take it easy, boy. Think on the bright side. You can enjoy this sanctuary with us. You don't need anything else. (Willy)

"You're right. Now we're finally free.

"Let's drink and eat in honor of this beautiful day. The day our beloved friends arrived here.

"Yes, that's a great reason for celebration. (Willy)

It's been a long night watered by food and strong drinks. The little gypsy fell asleep deeply in the cabin. With that, the outsiders took advantage of her and raped her.

"How? What's wrong? What happened? (Gypsy)

"I don't know, sister. All I know is those bastards got away. Do you want me to get back at them? (brother)

"No. I'll do it myself. I don't feel like living after what they did to me anymore. Furthermore, I'm delivering for the other world today. But my curse is for every man who approaches this place. That way, they'll respect me. I'm not a gypsy by chance.

The men who abused the girl died in mysterious accidents. From this day forward, the gypsy became a legend of Fernando of Noronha Island.

Roof man

At the general's house

In one of the few residences of Fernando of Noronha Island, were found General Felipe Moreira, his daughter Luiza and his wife Albertina.

Luiza

Dad, you look tired. What happened?

Felipe Moreira

I'm worried. I just got some dangerous bad guys in prison. They were deported from the mainland, and they don't seem friendly at all.

Albertina

What is it, man? Are you scared? You're the general here. Trust yourself.

Felipe Moreira

It's not like that, woman. My position isn't that comfortable. Dealing with this takes care.

Albertina

I see. I'll pray that everything's okay.

Luiza

I'll do that too, Mom.

Felipe Moreira

I leave that assignment to you. Furthermore, I'm not one to believe in that kind of stuff. I'm more attached to science and politics.

Luiza

We know, Dad. Don't worry. You can go to work. We'll be fine.

Felipe Moreira

I'll be right there, daughter. Be at peace.

Federal prison

The general enters the prison, but he feels something strange. From behind, three men arrest him, and he doesn't sketch reaction.

Felipe Moreira

What are you doing? What's going to happen?

Ezekiel

We are the resistance, old man! We're happy with this opportunity of reaction. Furthermore, we don't accept your rules! We want to be free, indeed and rightfully free. But you won't accept us! You arrest us because we broke the law, but we just want some peace! You have no right to decide our lives!

Roger

You represent oppression and discrimination to us. Furthermore, you're our opponent. We will have no mercy on you or the government because they have no consideration for us. This is our moment of revenge!

Andrade

Did you know you're going to die? You'll pay for your mistake. We're not the ones who are paying. One day, it's hunting and another day it's the hunters.

Felipe Moreira

I'm just a simple employee. I'm a lawman and obligations. You may even kill me, but that's not going to erase what you did. I will not leave you alone in any time in your lives. You'll get change.

Ezekiel

You're full of shit.

The three men acted and strangled the general. His screams echo away until he dies. Grief remains on the island.

Burial

The family has gathered, mourned for the death of the general. They've come practically all relatives to say goodbye to this important government leader. They spent the whole day watching the body in the middle of prayer for their soul. Still, everyone wanted revenge.

The funeral march has moved to the cemetery. The time has come for the family's testimony:

Luiza

He was a model father. He did all his obligations. I've never missed anything. I had food, leisure, clothes, shoes and nice conversations. He was a remarkable father. He was polite, kind, and gentle. It was years of good emotions on your side. So, dad, go in peace. With you will be my prayers and prayers. I'll never forget the good father you were. I'll always be grateful for everything you've done for our family.

Aunt Bernice

He was a highly social man. An example of professional for everyone who admired him. He was very responsible for his family. He always visited us and supported us. Furthermore, he deserves the best credit at the time of death.

Albertina

He was the love of my life. We met at college in Recife. It was love at first sight. Since then, we've never been apart. We built a family together and a name of respect. I just have to thank you for 30 years of marriage.

Give it up for the general.

Screams one of the gifts in one last farewell act.

The night of revenge

The full moon night has arrived. Seven days after the General's death, his soul woke with a thirst for revenge. After setting up the rooftops, he reached the enemy's room. With his spiritual power, he set fire to the whole environment while the enemies were asleep.

They woke up being eaten by the flames. Before the suffering of rivals, the wolves laughed. The devil comes and carries all the tenant souls. Planned and successful revenge. A mixture of peace fills the general's family. His death had been avenged. Who iron hurts, with him will be hurt?

From this day on, the legend was created and terrorized the island residents.

The Giants of Fernando of Noronha

In the remote times, there was a rich, valuable kingdom on the island that dominated the entire South America's current region. It's about the Giants of Noronha. It was a society formed by giant men and women, connected to the mysticism of nature and religion. There were clear rules of narrow communion with the creator and obedience to the superiors.

But it was a society without love or without strong social relations. It lasted for centuries until something unexpected happened between a couple of giants.

Rodney

I don't know what it feels like, Grace. But I'm feeling something strange. It's a slipstream of emotions that dominates my entire body. I feel my heart pounding, my legs shake and I look forward to seeing you. During the day, my thoughts concentrate on knowing how you are. And at night, I'm imagining situations with you. It's almost a chemical dependence. I need to always be around you. I need to participate in your life somehow. Am I a sinner? I don't understand these laws we follow. They're such hard, meaningless laws. Why love someone far away and despise who is near? I feel like I need a human heat. Because I can't feel desires or like someone? Why this fixation on dominating the world? After I met you, none of this makes any sense to me. I prefer to feel exactly what I described. What do you think about it, my beloved?

Grace

That really sounds familiar. I feel something like this happening in my life. I'm feeling the need to look pretty, walk, be with you every moment. I feel dependent on your company and your protection. Your presence brings me a security that I've never felt with anyone. I know our law. But I'm not afraid of others. I think the risk is worth it. This discovery brings me peace and makes me distressed at the same time. Why can't we live this love? I think we're free. We need to try to find this explosion point we so deserve. We need to give our freedom cry once and for all.

Rodney

I agree with you. So, let's let this feeling guide us completely.

The lovers gave themselves their passion and discovered the carnal pleasures. When the others discovered the transgression of the law, they were sacrificed. The woman's breasts were ripped off and today became the Die of both brothers. The man's genital organ was also cut creating the Pico Die.

The Golden Pot Woman

The Island of Fernando of Noronha had always received numerous visits from pirates from all the places in the world. They say the place is full of buried treasures and filled with supernatural creatures. It's usually the souls of the pirates who died guarding the gold.

The island is a wonderful tourist spot because of its natural beauties. It's considered one of the most beautiful places in the world. Searching for a rest of his life assigned, businessman Andrew and his wife Meggie landed on the island.

The couple besides love traveling, they're a couple of treasure hunters. After having a lot of fun all day, they went out to walk in the middle of the night with only the moonlight and their pile flashlight.

Andrew

What a fantastic place! I'm loving this ride, my love. But, in fact, we should be professional. I want to get rich with the island treasures. I want to be able to have the life I've always dreamed of. We deserve it. We've always fought our whole lives.

Meggie

I agree, love. But let's be careful. The treasure owners might be bothered. We need to draw up a perfect strategy. I believe we're on the right track.

Andrew

Of course, we are. I've thought about everything. Nothing bad can happen to us.

In that, it appeared in their sight field a nasty old woman who presented herself:

Old

I'm hungry, gentlemen. Could you share with me the bread you have in the bag?

Meggie

Of course, I do, ma'am. Take these two buns. That'll ease your hunger.

Old

I'm very grateful for your charity. As a retribution, I'll give you my pet jar. I found this pot buried in one of the island places. I was waiting for the right person to give it to. See you later. Be with God.

The couple got pot. When opening it, they found several gold coins which represented a small fortune. It's like the saying goes, "The universe repays exactly what we offer him."

Midnight giant

On the bright moon nights, he usually appears in Fernando of Noronha a man of gigantic stature. Scratchy and wearing a fallen hat, the giant approached the beach and started fishing. Since his appearance, no one could fish anymore. By work of magic, all fish were drawn to the vessel of these illustrious figures.

If anyone tried to follow him or catch him, he'd follow his walk and disappear in the middle of the woods. Then he reappeared at another point on the island that he was more peaceful. The giant simply dominated fishing on the island and made everyone scared.

Finished fishing, the giant joined ghosts, goblins and fairies to throw a stirred party. With lots of dancing, music, sex and drugs they were called the Libertinage Group. Some of the island residents were delighted with this culture and also participated in the racket.

Parties lasted weeks or months. Then simply the giant was gone for a while. It was his hibernation period in the astral world. Because it was a magical place, the island was covering several spiritual dimensions. Their friends would go back to work and wait with anxiety for a new meeting that promised more emotions than last time. It's like the saying goes, life is made of moments and fun.

The lost treasure

Around the 16th century, he landed on the island one of the most feared pirates of the time. Francis Drake was a great pirate, riches rapper, rapist of women, child killer among other terrible things. Recently, he had stolen a ship and was being chased.

Astute, he seeks a safe place to bury his treasure. It was an incalculable wealth of coins, precious jewelry, gold bars and personal effects. He kept this treasure in one of the most inaccessible caves on the island.

Before he left the place, he cast a spell in the cave. So, the treasure was guarded by three supernatural creatures, a creature half ounce and half snake, a creature half crocodile and half dragon, a creature half man and half eagle. Everyone who tried to rescue the treasure was simply destroyed.

The crippled, teeth-free boy

Legend tells us John was a very naughty boy to his parents. All the advice he received, he disdained and continued his evil. The situation was getting worse that it's reached an unsustainable point. So, your stepfather reacted and gave him a pretty big beating that broke all his teeth and a leg. See you

After that day, the boy got sick and was sad. He spent three months between life and death until he finally passed away in consequence of the complications of the wound. As punishment for being such a bad boy, he became a soul-wrecked island. Every child who disobeys his parents and leaves in the middle of the night, he chases and frightens.

The Sea Monster

The southeast bay was a magical place. In the middle of the night, there was noises and deafening moans. They were terrible sea monsters that surrounded the island. They were creatures from the ancient city of Atlantis who appeared mysteriously. They were species of sharks, killer whales, snakes, giant crocodiles, among others.

The legend tells us Atlantic and Fernando of Noronha were part of the same astral government. It was Prince Tefeth's government, who ordered no stranger to approach his domain. These magical creatures were enchanted by their spell and were servants of their domain and power.

Anyone approached and tried to fish on the coast at that time was bewitched and had a terrible end. The mermaids sucked the victim's blood and shared with the fish, the remains of the flesh. So, each of you respect your limits and do not attempt to face the dominions of Prince Tefeth.

The Heavy Woman
forest

Man

I've been walking for days without rest. I can't stand it anymore. I'm going to have to spend the night here in the middle of these woods.

Flying fish

As the night falls, I'm preparing my dinner. The fish will be delicious. It's very healthy food.

meditating

It's fearful to stay here, but I have no choice. I'm going to have to get over my fear because I'm in a place full of legends and fantasies.

eating

The food really looks delicious. I'm glad I learned how to cook since I was young.

kill

I already ate! I'm pretty tired. I'll try to sleep now

Heavy woman

I'll choke you! You won't survive!

Man

You're the fool! Your hat is mine!

Heavy woman

Please give me back my hat.

Man

Of course, I'll give it back. But you have to fulfill my wish.

Heavy woman

What do you want?

Man

I'm very poor. I want to get rich.

Heavy woman

Very well. I grant your wish. You'll be the richest man in the region.

Man

Thank you. I'll enjoy life with a lot of money. That's all I ever wanted. Nice doing business with you, Heavy Woman.

The haunted house

Son

Mom, this house is so weird. I see noise of breaking dishes, doors being scratched, steps, lightning torches flying and ghosts. I'm so scared!

Mommy

Calm down, son, you must be a suffering spirit. The former residents of this house were witches. Some spiritual work of their trapped this poor spirit.

Son

How can I help you?

Mommy

Next time the spirit comes, you talk to him. Have courage and help this poor creature.

Son

Okay. I promise I'll try to do it.

Mommy

You're a good young man. It's Mom's pride.

Son

You're my pride, too. Thanks for the guidance.

Room

young

You came. How can I help you?

Ghost

Thanks for the interest, kid. But I don't want your help. This is my house and I want you to leave. I promise I won't hurt you if you obey me.

Young

But why do we bother?

Ghost

I don't have to explain. I just want you to leave.

Young

Okay. I'll pray for you.

Ghost

Don't do that. I'm a fallen angel. I don't want it, and I don't want the light. Leave me alone.

Young

Thy will be done!

The Wolf

room

Mom

Son, go shopping at the supermarket because the pantry is empty.

Son

I won't, Mama. I'm busy. If you want, go get it yourself.

Mom

How ungrateful! Don't you remember everything I do for you?

Son

You do it because you want to. Each one who takes care of his own responsibilities.

Kitchen

Mom

Son, I've been told about you. Is it true you're asking for alms on the street?

Son

Yes, it's true. I'm bound to do this because you don't give me money.

Mom

I'm not obliged to give you money. You're a boy already. If you want money, go to work!

Son

Why don't you like me? I'm your only son and you don't value me.

Mom

I love you. But you embarrass me all the time. I don't approve of your attitudes.

Son

Ordinary! I'll teach you a lesson!

Son beats his mother

Mom

Damn you! Why did you hit me, I hide you! From now on, you'll lie on the grass like an animal. You'll be a wolf!

Mom

Now, you're a lesson to all the rebel children. Respect for parents is God's law. You'll never be a man again because you beat your own mother.

The monster of the forest

Mommy

Honey, there's no wood. Could you get it for me?

Wife

Woman, it's night. Why didn't you ask first?

Mommy

I didn't even notice the lack of wood. Don't tell me you're scared. A man this big! Shame on you!

Wife

It's not fear! It's just a precaution. But if it's urgent, I'll take my chances!

Mommy

That's why I love you, baby.

Man

Being in nature is something really incredible and dangerous. Night falls and makes the forest look even more mysterious. How nice to be a part of this! The owner of all this is God. Some are people feel proud, but they don't own anything. We're just dust and dust we'll return. So, love it intensely.

I have a beautiful wife. It was the woman my dreams could conquer. I even do crazy things for her. An example is to be here in the woods running dangers. I hope I get out of this alive!

Man

I found the wood. Now I'm going home!

A monster! Oh, my God!

Home

Woman

What's up, man? Why are you desperate?

Man

I saw a monster! I shouldn't have listened to you! I almost got screwed.

Woman

Oh, my God! How awful! How could I guess, my love? I just wanted the wood. Thanks for trying! I forgive you for that!

Man

Do you still forgive me? How sarcastic! But that's okay. As much as I love you, I'll never go to the woods at night again. You're not even asking me.

Woman

No problem! The important thing is that our love remains. You are my gold, my love.

Man

You're important to me too. I forgive you!

The Pearl Island in Polynesia

After hours of crossing the revolting sea, the serial team approaches an island. It was dark and they were blurry and fatigued. They settle it then dock it on the island.

Divine

We're finally here! I was tired of the great crossing at sea. With this, new hopes rise. I'm very excited for this new learning stage.

Renato

Me too, dear fellow adventure. Anxiety defines me completely. The sea crossing was interesting and invigorating. But I want more emotions and adventures.

Guardian

We'll have more learning, for sure. This seems like a nice island to me. A place to rest and reflect. Let's hope we find a sign of life.

Alexis

They just found it. I'm an island manager. My name is Alexis. Who are you?

Divine

I am the son of God. But they also know me as psychic or Divine. We're on vacation expedition. Fate brought us here.

Renato

My name is Renato. I'm an integral of the psychic's team. I love fantastic adventures.

Guardian

I am the spirit of the mountain. I'm the team advisor. It's an honor to be here. We're tired. Could you help us?

Alexis

You can count on my help. Come with me. My house is near here.

The quartet starts walking on the island beach. Next thing you know, they're in the closed woods. Through the guide, in a few minutes, they can reach a simple, rustic cabin with a view of the sea. That's all they needed at that moment. They enter the inside of the house and settle in the room.

Divine

Could you tell us where exactly we are?

Alexis

You're on Pitcairn Island in Polynesia.

Renato

That's wonderful. Could you tell your short story?

Alexis

Humans have been on this island for over a millennium. They used to use this island and the neighboring island known as Henderson. From the beginning, the inhabitants of the two islands cooperated with each other creating a solid trade. However, there was an environmental disaster in the 16th century that impossibly communication between the islands. About a hundred years later, the islands were rediscovered by the English. We became British colony in 1838. Actually, few people live here.

Guardian

Living on an island must be highly challenging. What's your economy consistent with?

Alexis

We have a very fertile soil. We planted lots of fruit, vegetables and grain. We fish and do crafts, too. We are also a country of mineral riches. We produced a lot of precious metals.

Divine

How does your communication work with the world?

Alexis

We have access to television, radio and Internet. Definitely the modern world has arrived on our island.

Renato

How's your way of living? What do you believe?

Alexis

In ancient times, we followed very strict rules. But with globalization, we're totally liberal. We believe in God.

Guardian

Are there ghosts around here?

Alexis

Lots of ghosts. The oldest houses are haunted by several of them. We avoided going out at night in fear of the werewolf or the Giant Monkey.

Renato

Oh, my God! I'm so scared! Where did we go?

Divine

Very calm at that time, Renato. It's just one night we're going to be here. Nothing bad is going to happen.

Alexis

You have nothing to worry about. These monsters only appear on the full moon. You're safe.

Guardian

Good. We're calmer. It's going to be a great stay.

Alexis

Now it's my turn to ask. How did you get here? Who are you really?

Divine

I'm psychic. We came from Brazil. We're the main characters in the series the psychic. Over time, we're going to perform harder adventures. This is the part of the Adventures in the world. We've abandoned all our commitments so we can meet new cultures, places and beliefs. It's very instigating to travel, to feel, to learn and to help people. I believe every human being has its mission. Each one can play a good role by contributing to a better world. If I could give you some advice,

I'd say, "Love more, live more, forgive more." But also stay away from the bad influences. The wolf can't live with sheep. So put things together. Being happy is a matter of choice. You're not going to be a partner who's going to make you a chance. Be happy for yourself. Grow up and win. Be the lead in your own life.

Alexis

Well done, beloved. I've always been guided by good behavior. We learn from our parents the good values. You know, being away from urban violence is a big prize. It's like we're in heaven promised by Christ. Through our communications, we realize the world isn't going well. People forget God and live-in materialism. Evil is great and frightening. We need to breathe, rethink values and evolve. Nothing is by chance. We need to make a difference.

Guardian

Be that difference in people's lives. That's why we're here. Celebrate life.

Renato

Always be the change. Don't be happy to be just a common person. Use your good works and help the world.

Alexis

I will. Thank you, everyone.

A paradise in the middle of the sea

The psychic's troupe sails into the sea. A blast of winds followed by a thin breeze hits the ship. It's time for a lot of team concentration.

Divine

The night is falling. We've been sailing through the sea for hours, but no sign of life. I'm losing hope. What's waiting for us?

Guardian

Easy, dreamer. It takes patience and hope. We'll be getting close to some island in a few minutes. I'm sensing that everything will get better. Believe it.

Renato

You're the one who taught us to take precaution and faith. Don't let me down, dear friend. Let's keep trying.

Divine

Okay. You guys convinced me. Let's move on.

Two hours later, they finally arrive at the Coconut Archipelago. A lush landscape shows itself in your eyes. The islands are covered by a rainforest. Many animals, rich vegetation and sea species. Mountains, high ground and large quantities of coconuts characterize the relevance.

Guardian

We came to rest. It seems to me a very mystical place. I feel intense positive vibrations. What do you think, son of God?

Divine

It's a lovely place. I feel good here. What about you, Renato?

Renato

It's like a place of my dreams. Rich nature, good weather and mystery. That's all I wanted.

Jasmine

Good night, everyone. Where do you come from and what do you want?

Divine

I'm the psychic. We're a team of adventurers and we're looking for adventure. And you?

Jasmine

I'm the island administrator. I see you're tired from the trip. I offer you food and rest.

Guardian

Thank you so much! So, we can get to know each other better.

The four of them moved to the meters to a rustic house. Small but comfortable residence. They've entered the place accommodating on the couch in the living room.

Divine

Thank you so much for staying. Could you tell us a little bit about the story of this place?

Jasmine

It'll be an honor. The island was discovered in the early 17th century by a British captain belonging to the Indian company. But soon he left and the island remained uninhabited. Two centuries later, a Scottish sailor arrived here who fixed residence. After successful changes of command, the territory currently belongs to Australia.

Renato

How's the economy of this place?

Jasmine

We produce coconut and copra and import the rest of the products.

Guardian

How's the weather here?

Jasmine

Climate is good, rain and suitable sun. In the first few months of the year, we've been in cyclones action. But overall, it's really nice to live here.

Divine

Do we have legends here?

Jasmine

Several. There are reports of people who have seen ghosts. Many sailors died here in remote times. But I honestly don't believe that. I've never seen anything unusual.

Guardian

True or not, it's a highly interesting place. We're on an unprecedented trip. We need to know the world to understand ourselves. We want to know our place in the world. In every place we've landed, new emotions. That's why it's so important to you guys.

Jasmine

I'm glad I'm contributing. You've already left your mark. You're nice, intelligent and spiritualistic. It's a pleasure to have you.

Renato

I thank you on behalf of everyone. This is becoming quite interesting. That contributes to our knowledge. Let's never forget these moments.

Jasmine

Make yourselves comfortable. Now, you're part of the island history. I'll miss you when you leave.

Divine

That's inevitable. We're citizens of the world. We carry good experiences and forget the bad experiences. It's an evolutionary process of the soul. Your help is very good. Let's rest. The next adventure promises.

On the island of Ascension

The psychic's troupe has been traveling through the ocean in company of the Portuguese Navigator John of Nova. It was moments of great anguish and excitement due to the turns of the journey.

John of Nova

We're approaching Ascension Island. We need to stop to refuel. We need to find food, fuel, and rest the ship's instruments. There's a natural wear of all the components of the ship. How do you feel, young dreamers?

Divine

We're doing great. Glad you got a break. We're so bored with this trip. We also need to refuel our spiritual energy, balance the opposite forces, control the chakras, implode the inner aura and give our cry of freedom. What do you think, master?

Spirit of the Mountain

It's a rendezvous point of our goals. Destiny calls us to reflect, question ourselves about everything we've been through, experiencing new situations. In short, adventures call us to act. I feel positive vibrations from everyone who accompanies us. How do you feel, Renato?

Renato

I feel totally happy to know about the land. I am an earthly being by nature.

John of Nova

Very well. I'm happy for all of us. Let's move on.

The arrival to the island

The sailors are landing. The sun is strong and the winds form a thin breeze in the southeast direction of the island. Since the weather was good, they start building a simple cabin. Soon after, the shelter is ready.

Renato

I'm seriously thinking about walking the island. Sounds like a nice place.

Divine

I'm feeling it too. I haven't been on a walk-in day. The ship's environment is not proper for physical exercises. We know how important this is to the body.

Spirit of the Mountain

Then I propose a press conference walk. Although it's a good retrospect, we don't know what secrets the island keeps. Precaution must be the main point to be observed at this point.

John of Nova

I'll walk you out. Don't worry. I'm a very experienced man.

They did as they agreed. They started a joint walk along the island trails. The place was characterized by the creepy, dry, sterile vegetation. In their company, goats, cows and horses that grazed. On the coast, there were sea birds and turtles.

The walk begins to slow steps. The sun was cautious what caused sweats and exhaustion.

John of Nova

I made a point of keeping up with you guys for safety. We don't know we can find it here.

Spirit of the Mountain

Whatever happens, we're prepared, sir. We're a competent team in adventures. It seems that danger is always within our grasp. In my millennia of experience, I learned to face the situations very lightly.

Renato

My foster mom is genius. I learned important things from you, Mom. I'm a more confident person around you.

Mountain spirit

I'm glad, son. I love this mission of being your false mother.

Divine

I admire your union. I'm more experienced and complete because I live with both. This is extremely important to my literary career.

John of Nova

Oh, man! I'm overwhelmed by your ability. We're in the right place and at the right time. We came to shine!

They cross a lot of the island. Near an abyss, they stop a little to observe the characteristic landscape of the place. Right now, a tall, strong, manly, dark old man presents himself.

Island protector

I'm the protector of the island. Could you explain why you came to visit?

John of Nova

We've come on a mission of peace. We're resting a long trip.

Island protector

All right! But I'm asking you to leave as soon as possible. This place is my territory. I don't like being disturbed by anyone.

Spirit of the Mountain

We understand perfectly. Don't worry about it. We'll leave tomorrow.

Divine

We're good people. We're not going to hurt you. Can you tell me why all this fear?

Island protector

It's nothing against you. But I was a vicious sorcerer. If anyone stays on the island for more than seven days, I just disappear. So, I ask for everyone's cooperation.

Renato

No problem, buddy. We won't get in the way of you.

As the master promised, they retired from the island and returned to the ship. There were still many things to experience in their walks around the world.

The end